MW01027935

cornbread & poppy
at the carnival

matthew cordell

LB

Little, Brown and Company
New York Boston

To Romy and Dean

About This Book

The illustrations for this book were done in pen and ink with watercolor. The series is designed by Joann Hill. The text was set in New Century Schoolbook, and the display type is hand lettered.

This book is a work of fiction. Names, characters, places, and incidents are the product of the author's imagination or are used fictitiously. Any resemblance to actual events, locales, or persons, living or dead, is coincidental.
• Copyright © 2022 by Matthew Cordell • Cover art copyright © 2022 by Matthew Cordell. • Cover design by Joann Hill, David Hastings, and Lynn El-Roeiy. • Cover copyright © 2022 by Hachette Book Group, Inc. • Hachette Book Group supports the right to free expression and the value of copyright. The purpose of copyright is to encourage writers and artists to produce the creative works that enrich our culture. • The scanning, uploading, and distribution of this book without permission is a theft of the author's intellectual property. If you would like permission to use material from the book (other than for review purposes), please contact permissions@hbgusa.com. Thank you for your support of the author's rights. • Little, Brown and Company • Hachette Book Group • 1290 Avenue of the Americas, New York, NY 10104 • Visit us at LBYR.com • First Edition: June 2022 • Little, Brown and Company is a division of Hachette Book Group, Inc. • The Little, Brown name and logo are trademarks of Hachette Book Group, Inc. • The publisher is not responsible for websites (or their content) that are not owned by the publisher. • Library of Congress Cataloging-in-Publication Data • Names: Cordell, Matthew, 1975– author, illustrator. • Other titles: Cornbread and Poppy at the carnival • Title: Cornbread & Poppy at the carnival / Matthew Cordell. • Other titles: Cornbread and Poppy at the carnival • Description: First edition. | New York : Little, Brown and Company, 2022. | Series: Cornbread and Poppy ; [2] | Audience: Ages 6-10. | Summary: Best friends Cornbread and Poppy spend a day at the Carnival playing games, eating snacks, and riding the Ferris wheel. • Identifiers: LCCN 2021038903 | ISBN 9780759554894 (hardcover) | ISBN 9780759554900 (paperback) | ISBN 9780316168991 (ebook) | ISBN 9780759554887 (ebook other) • Subjects: CYAC: Mice—Fiction. | Best friends—Fiction. | Friendship—Fiction. | Carnivals—Fiction. • Classification: LCC PZ7.C815343 Cq 2022 | DDC [E]—dc23 • LC record available at https://lccn.loc.gov/2021038903 • ISBNs: 978-0-7595-5489-4 (hardcover), 978-0-7595-5490-0 (pbk.), 978-0-316-16899-1 (ebook), 978-0-316-40057-2 (ebook), 978-0-316-40077-0 (ebook) • Printed in China • APS • Hardcover: 10 9 8 7 6 5 4 3 2 • Paperback: 10 9 8 7 6 5 4 3 2

Contents

❧ The Best News Ever ❧

Cornbread was hungry. His best friend, Poppy, was eleven minutes late for lunch.

"Cornbread, I have the best news!" said Poppy, finally arriving at his door. Cornbread loved Poppy, but he always worried when she had "the best news."

"Come in, Poppy," Cornbread said. "The last time you had the best news, we saw that terrible movie you wanted to see. I had nightmares for a week."

SCREAM!!

Cornbread was afraid of monsters.

"The time before that when you had the best news, we ate that terrible runny cheese you wanted to eat. It upset my stomach for hours."

Cornbread was afraid of runny cheese.

"And the time before that when you had the best news, we explored the old Crawdad Caverns…

...and I fainted."

Cornbread was afraid of the dark.

"Okay, fine! But not all my news makes you sick and scared, Cornbread!" said Poppy. It was true. Poppy often had news of things that didn't end terribly.

Like snacking on raspberries at Grandma Winkle's farm.

Like sailing down Whipple Creek

on rubber ducks.

Like dancing to the Marmot Band at the big town Barn Buster.

"Okay," Cornbread allowed.

"What is it?"

13

14

"The Carnival is in town!" shouted Poppy.

"What's the Carnival?" asked Cornbread.

Poppy was surprised. "You've never been to the Carnival?!"

"At the Carnival, there's sweets and treats...."

"Mmm...sweets and treats," said Cornbread.

"Games and prizes…"

"I do like games," said Cornbread.

"There's even high-flying, zooming rides!"

"Uh-oh," said Cornbread.

"Uh-oh?" said Poppy.

"I am not going to zoom, and I am not going to fly! That sounds terribly big and terribly fast, and just one wrong turn and we're... SQUOOSH."

"Oh, Cornbread," said Poppy. "There is no SQUOOSH. These rides are operated by professionals. And anyway, I'll protect you!"

"You will?" asked Cornbread.

21

"Of course! Remember when you were scared after that movie? I slept by your bed for a week."

"Well, yes..."

"And when that fabulous runny cheese didn't agree with you? I made you ginger tea and sang you sweet lullabies till you were better."

"Well, yes..."

"And remember when you fainted in the old Crawdad Caverns? I carried you all the way out on my back."

"Hmm. Yes, I do remember that, Poppy," said Cornbread. "Thank you for protecting me."

"And thank you for doing new things with me!" said Poppy. "So... to the Carnival?"

"To the Carnival!" Cornbread agreed.

"That's the best news ever!"

"But first...lunch!" said Cornbread.

The Carnival

"Wow, the whole town must be here!" Poppy
exclaimed.

Down at the base of Maggie Valley, there were tents and booths and great big mechanical moving structures. Animals of all kinds swarmed in and around it all.

"Let's get down there and see the Carnival, Cornbread!"

At the entrance, they paid two hay pennies
to a badger to get in.

Inside, they saw both familiar and
not-so-familiar faces.

An elephant family
was snacking on
a gigantic bag of
roasted peanuts.

Sable and Horsefeather
were waiting in line for
cotton candy.

Cornbread and Poppy were
surprised to see that even
Old Larry, the town grump, had
pulled himself out of bed to visit the Carnival.

"Wouldn't miss it!" said Old Larry, munching
a fried apple fritter.

"Let's get a fritter, Cornbread!" said Poppy.

Cornbread had never even heard of a fritter.
But it smelled and looked delicious.

"Yum!" Cornbread said. It was warm and buttery, sweet and crispy on the outside and soft on the inside.

"Step right up!" barked a pig from a nearby booth. "Every player is a winner!"

Poppy paid the pig, and she was given three rings to toss and try to land on a bottle.

One...

Two...

Three...

"Every player is a winner!" barked the pig,
and he gave Poppy a dented bottle cap.

"Not much of a winner," said
Poppy, a little less happy than
before.

35

"Let me try," said Cornbread.
"I do love games."

He paid the pig.

One...

Two...

Three...

"Every player is a winner!" barked the pig, and he gave Cornbread a giant plush banana.

"For you, Poppy." Cornbread smiled,
giving Poppy his prize.

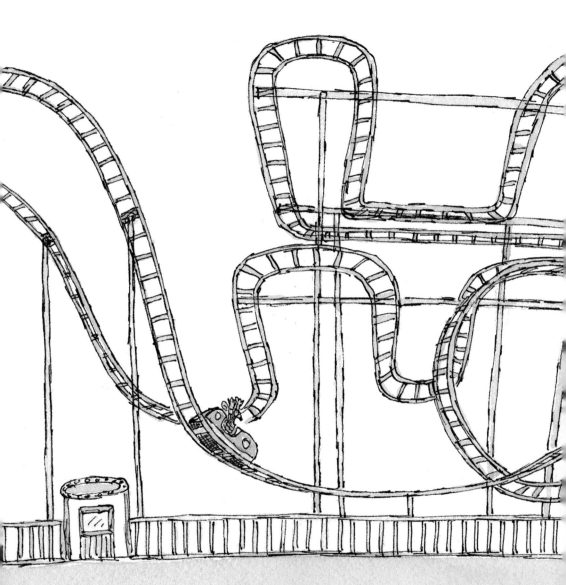

A roller coaster zoomed by on some nearby tracks. "Uh-oh," said Cornbread.

"Let's go on the Boneshaker!"
Poppy exclaimed.

BONESHAKER

"No way," said Cornbread.

41

"Want to ride
the Nauseator?"
asked Poppy.

"Not a chance,"
said Cornbread.

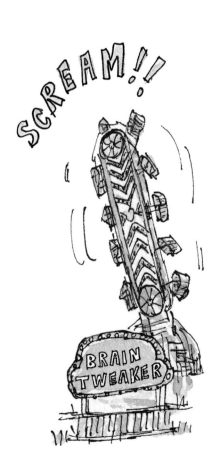

"How about the
Brain Tweaker?"

"Nope."

"Will you please ride one ride with me, Cornbread? What about the Ferris wheel over there?"

"Well...a Ferris wheel sounds nice and calm. I will ride that with you, Poppy."

They walked to the other side of the Carnival.

"It's huge!" cried Cornbread.

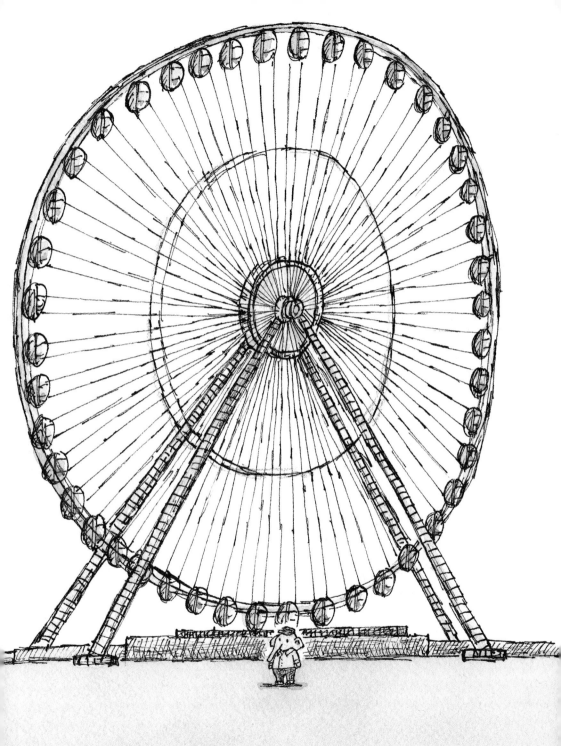

"Elephant-size!" said the elephant operator.

Cornbread and Poppy climbed into the giant gondola. They pulled their seat belts tight.

The wheel began to turn, and
they rose higher…

...and higher
off the ground.

But surprisingly...

Cornbread wasn't afraid.
The ride was smooth and
slow, and he had never
seen the town from this
high up. It was amazing!

"Poppy, look! You can see
Grandma Winkle's farm!"

He looked over at Poppy.
Her eyes were closed.

"Poppy, look! Whipple Creek!"

Poppy screwed her eyes closed even tighter.

"Poppy! There's the old Crawdad Caverns!"

"Cornbread!" Poppy yelled.

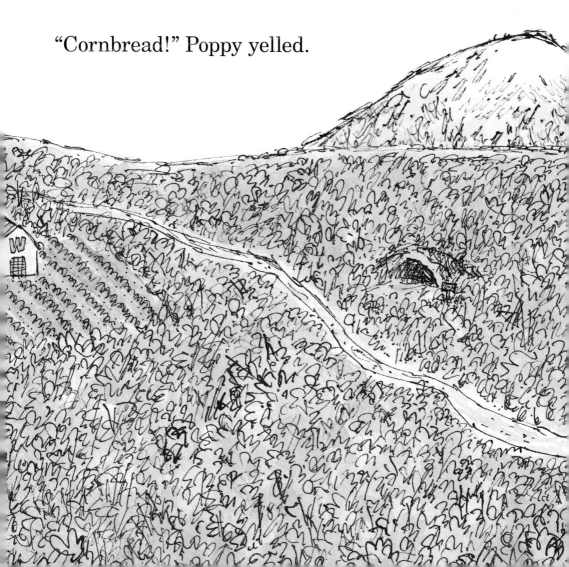

FERRIS
WHEEL

... I'm scared of heights!

heights!

heights!

Cornbread reached over. He squeezed
Poppy's hand.

"I'll protect you, Poppy," he said.

They rode around a few more times until the
wheel stopped.

"Thank you, Cornbread," said Poppy.

"You're welcome, Poppy," said Cornbread.
"I like the Carnival! I like rides!"

"Great! Let's go on the Gutbuster!"
shouted Poppy.

"Not a chance," said Cornbread.

 The Peanut

As they were about to leave the Carnival,
Cornbread noticed something.

"Poppy, look, there's a peanut by your bike."

59

"You bought me a peanut, Cornbread?" asked Poppy. "Thank you! I love peanuts!"

"I love peanuts too, Poppy. But I didn't buy it," Cornbread said. "It was just...there."

"Oh, goody! I can't wait to eat it. I'm starved,"
Poppy said.

Cornbread was starved too.

"Actually…," Cornbread decided, "I think I should have the peanut. I'm the one who found it, after all."

"Yes, Cornbread, but it was by MY bike. Whoever left it wanted ME to have it."

Poppy reached for the peanut.

"Yes, but maybe…," Cornbread said, stopping his friend, "someone just put it down here so they could rest for a minute. It is a big peanut. We should wait to see if someone comes back for it."

They waited.

For ten seconds.

"Okay, they aren't coming back. So, since I found the peanut, I think I should have the peanut."

"No, Cornbread, it's MY peanut!"

Then things got worse.

Poppy yelled and screamed about how much she loved peanuts and about all the ways she could prepare the peanut, and why SHE—not HE—deserved the peanut.

Then Cornbread yelled and
screamed about how he loved
peanuts and about how he was
just a baby mouse when he first
had a peanut and how he was
the one to introduce Poppy to
peanuts when they were just baby
mice, and because of that HE—not
SHE—deserved the peanut.

And they went back and forth and back and forth about the peanut until...

Poppy stormed off.

Cornbread stormed off.

Ten seconds passed.

Poppy was alone.

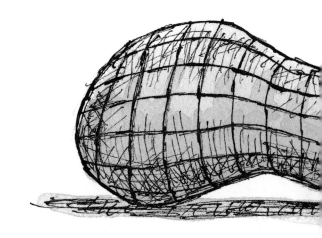

Cornbread was alone.

They both looked back at the peanut.

Inside the shell, there were two nuts....

Outside the shell, there were two friends....

"Hi, Cornbread."

"Hi, Poppy."

"Can we split it?" they both said.

Cornbread hugged Poppy, and Poppy hugged
Cornbread.

"Sharing will make it taste better!"
said Poppy.

A mighty elephant trunk sucked up
the peanut.

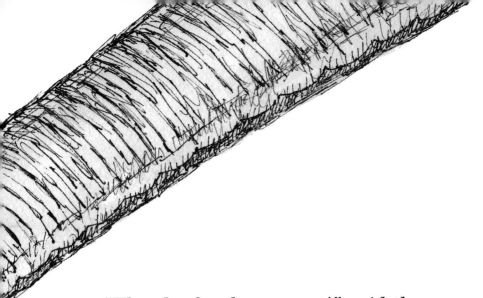

"Thanks for the peanut!" said the
Ferris wheel operator. "See you next year
at the Carnival!"

Poppy sighed.

Cornbread sighed.

"Do you want to get some cheese, Poppy?
They have the kind you like."

"Yes, please."

Poppy ordered the runny kind.

Cornbread got the cheddar.